Poofin
THE CLOUD THAT CRIED ON CHRISTMAS

Written by Richard M. Wainwright
Illustrations by Jack Crompton

Dedicated to D'Ann and Joanne
Richard M. Wainwright and Jack Crompton

**FAMILY LIFE
PUBLISHING**

Family Life Publishing
Dennis, Massachusetts 02638

Printed in Singapore by Tien Wah Press

Published in the United States of America 1989
Fourth Edition ISBN 0-9619566-1-5

Poofin

THE CLOUD THAT CRIED ON CHRISTMAS

Written by Richard M. Wainwright
Illustrations by Jack Crompton

To: _Katie_

*May Poofin
watch over you and
your family always!*

With best wishes
Richard M. Wainwright

From: _Grandma and Grandpa
Kelly with love!_

Best wishes –
your friend,
Richard M. Wainwright
1996

THE BELL FINALLY RANG. One more day of school until Christmas! Bobby waved goodbye to his friends. Even though he was young he was able to walk to school in good weather. He liked to walk, but most of all he enjoyed visiting with special friends.

At the top of the hill there were several white houses with balconies and porches. Wooden benches were scattered over the lawns. Many of the retired people who lived in the houses were sitting on benches or strolling along the walkways.

Mr. McGonigal spotted Bobby first. "Hi, Bobby," he called. "How was school today?"

"School was fine, thank you," Bobby replied.

"It's getting cold. Mr. McGonigal, do you think maybe we might have snow this year?" Bobby had asked this question many times, for he had never seen snow. In fact, none of the children of Peacedale had ever seen snow. Sleds, toboggans and skis gathered dust in boxes, attics and garages. Mr. McGonigal often spoke of the snow storms which came when he had been a boy.

Bobby would listen with a sad smile as Mr. McGonigal described sledding down Apple Hill and making huge snowmen and igloos with his friends.

No one knew why snow had stopped coming to Peacedale. The townspeople only knew how disappointed they were when winter passed without it.

"See you tomorrow," Bobby said to Mr. McGonigal as he started down the hill. Soon he came to an iron fence. As always, there was Carla with her long neck lowered over the gate waiting

for Bobby to scratch her head or hopefully give her a carrot. Carla was a bactrian ... a two-hump camel. She was one of the animals on Mr. Brown's farm.

Other animals came to the fence to greet Bobby. There was a llama, sheep, goats, a donkey, deer, cows, pigs, ducks and chickens. All the animals you would find on most farms and a few you wouldn't. Every animal had a name. The children in the town loved to visit Mr. Brown's farm and feed the animals, and Mr. Brown loved the children.

From Mr. Brown's farm it was only a few minutes to Bobby's house. He ran up the steps and in the side door to the kitchen. After a hug and a kiss from his mother, Bobby would sit by the kitchen window eating cookies and drinking milk, watching clouds drifting high in the sky.

To Bobby, some of the clouds looked like houses, others looked like animals, planes, trains, or even faces. One minute a cloud was a clown - the next a bird. They were a lot of fun to watch as the cookies disappeared.

"COME CLOSER, POOFIN," boomed a deep baritone voice. "Nebulous, supervisor of all small clouds, has reported that you spend all your days floating hither and yon, helping no one on earth."

A small fluffy white, roly-poly cloud moved near the bottom of a large thunderhead. He waited for Altos to speak again.

"Poofin," Altos continued, a little more gently, "we are responsible for caring for the planet below. With shade we protect the land, people and animals from too much sun. Our tears of sadness or joy provide the water every living creature needs to exist on earth. That is why, when there are not enough clouds, life in some places suffers. You have work to do - much to give. What do you have to say for yourself?"

Poofin thought a moment and nervously began in almost a whisper, "Oh, Altos, when I look below at the earth, I see only a blur of pretty greens, blues and browns. Maybe when I am older I will see better. I can't see people or places that need me, so I just float about changing my shape all day."

"I see," Altos interrupted. "In time your sight will improve, but we need your help now. I am going to send you to earth for a short visit. You will be able to talk with one human being. Maybe if you learn a little about life on earth, you will take your responsibilities more seriously. Be very careful with the power which allows you to change yourself because on earth you will also be able to change all things."

Bobby wiped his mouth after finishing the last cookie, got up and headed for his room to change into play clothes. He pushed open the door and began to walk toward his desk. What he saw caused him to stop, freeze and drop his books. There floating above the lamp on his desk was a smiling, chubby white cloud.

Bobby turned to run. "Please don't go ... I can't harm you" pleaded Poofin. Poofin's words sounded like the whispering of a spring breeze, but Bobby understood. "You can T-A-L-K," stammered Bobby as he slowly sat down on his bed. "Yes, Bobby, I can talk, but you alone on earth can understand my words. I can also change my shape." Poofin began to become thin with long skinny arms.

"No, no!" cried Bobby. "Don't change your shape. You're fine just the way you were."

Poofin returned to his original shape. "My name is Poofin. Altos, ruler of all clouds, sent me to learn about life on earth. Your window was open a crack ... so here I am. May I spend a few days with you?"

Bobby smiled. He was no longer afraid of this strange creature. "No one will believe me ..."

"You are right," Poofin interrupted, "no one will believe you. Others will see only a small white wispy cloud."

"Yes, Poofin, you can stay - I am glad to be your friend," said Bobby. "Maybe I can help you learn what you need to know."

Just then Bobby's mother called from the kitchen, "Don't forget to wrap your presents before you go out."

"I won't, Mom - I am going to do them right now," Bobby replied.

Bobby walked to a shelf and picked up a can of nuts and a large box of candy and carried them to his desk. Poofin floated a little bit higher and watched.

Beside Bobby's desk was a package of brightly colored paper and a roll of scotch tape. With scissors from the desk he began to cut the paper.

"What are you doing?" questioned Poofin.

"Wrapping Christmas presents," Bobby replied.

"What are Christmas presents?" Poofin asked.

"They are gifts - things we give other people," Bobby explained.

"But why do you give gifts?" Poofin responded.

Bobby smiled. "Hundreds of years ago a very special child was born and people from all parts of the world, rich and poor, came to see Him and they brought Him gifts."

"Is there more? Can you tell me more?" asked Poofin.

Bobby finished wrapping the two presents. They were far from perfect, but he knew his father and mother would be pleased because he had done it all by himself.

"I have a large picture book which explains the story of Christmas. If we look at it together, I think you will understand." As Bobby slowly turned the pages of the book, Poofin contentedly hovered above Bobby's shoulder, listening to the story.

The next morning Bobby put the presents in his school backpack. He told Poofin he would return in the afternoon. In the kitchen, his mother had his breakfast ready. Along with Bobby's lunch in his backpack, she put a plastic bag filled with carrots. Bobby bundled up because each day was becoming colder, and then he started off to school.

This was the last day of school before the Christmas vacation. Before leaving, Bobby gave a can of nuts to his teacher, Mrs. Thompson. On the way home he stopped to give Mr. McGonigal and his friends a box of candy.

Mr. McGonigal and some of the other men were busy constructing a large wooden stable on the lawn. It was a dearly loved tradition in Peacedale that on Christmas Eve the children of the town would walk in a procession that ended in front of Mr. McGonigal's stable. A few of Mr. Brown's animals would be tethered around the living creche and other pets would come with the children. Mothers, fathers and grandparents would wait and watch with children who were too young to join in the procession. At midnight the procession would arrive and everyone would join in the singing of Christmas carols, welcoming the most joyous day of the year.

"Guess what, Mr. McGonigal," said Bobby as he handed him his Christmas present.

"My guess is it's a box of old bananas - but we thank you anyhow," said Mr. McGonigal with smile.

Bobby laughed. "That's not what I meant. This year, Mr. Brown is going to let me ride Carla in the procession!"

"That's terrific, Bobby- we'll be here waiting for you. Oh, and Bobby, thank you for the candy."

A few minutes later, Bobby had finished giving Carla and the other animals their Christmas carrots. Bobby hurried home remembering that Poofin would be waiting.

"Can I take my milk and cookies to my room, Mom?" Bobby asked.

"Of course, but please don't forget to bring the glass and the plate back to the kitchen," his mother replied.

Bobby edged his door open with his elbow and stepped into his room. One look and he almost dropped his cookies and milk.

A beaming Poofin hovered near the back wall. "I changed things a little bit. Do you like it?" he asked.

Bobby's bed was now 'V' shaped, with high legs on either end. His desk was two levels. Shelves were slanted so that all the books were piled at one end. Bobby's baseball glove had eight fingers and his favorite baseball bat was so big he knew he couldn't even lift it.

"Oh, Poofin," Bobby lamented, "this is awful ... I can't sleep in a bed like that ... people must lie flat. I can't select a book because they are piled on top of each other. I have only four fingers and a thumb, so my glove is ruined, and I will certainly not be able to swing that huge bat."

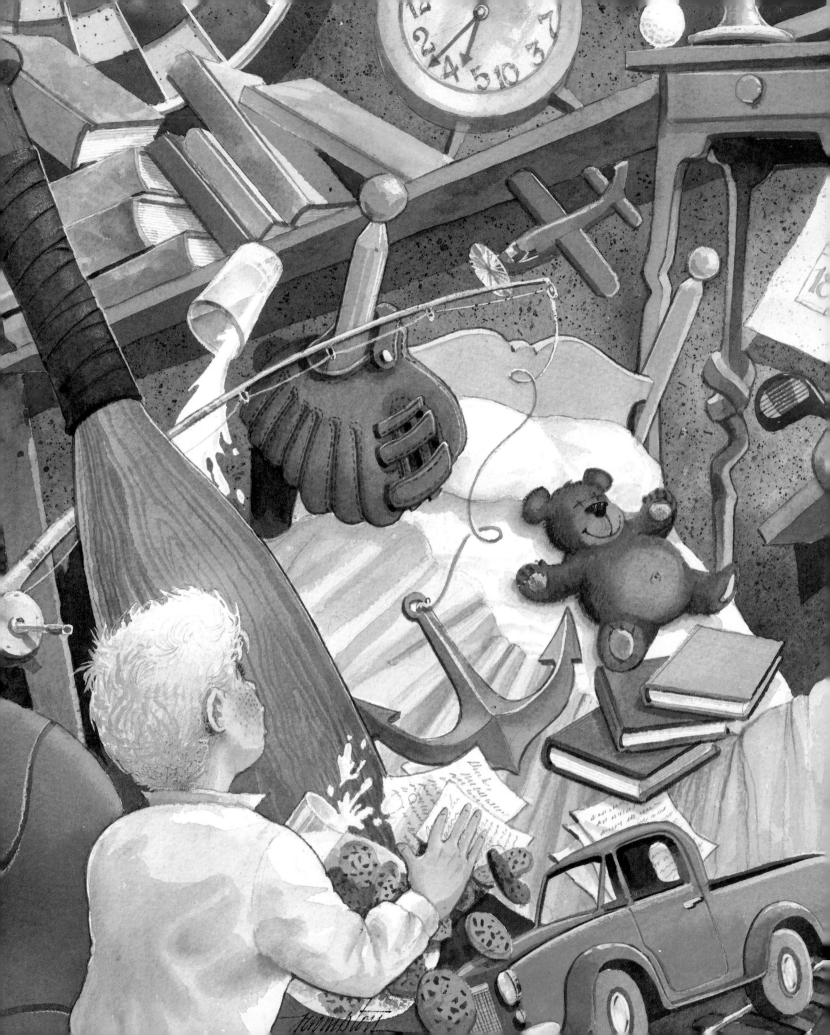

"I just wanted to do something for you," said Poofin, "for allowing me to stay."

"Yes, Poofin, I understand, but won't you please make my room just the way it was?"

Poofin nodded sadly and closed his eyes. Everything began to change. Soon Bobby was able to sit down at his desk and eat his cookies.

"Poofin, I must go shopping to buy two more gifts. One for my mother and father and one to carry with me in the Christmas procession. Do you want to come with me?"

Poofin's face brightened and he quickly flattened out, drifting out the slightly open window.

Bobby waved to his animal friends as he walked quickly past Mr. Brown's farm. Poofin followed along above him. Strings of brightly colored lights crisscrossed above the streets in the shopping area. Christmas wreaths decorated the doors of stores and behind their large windows, gifts were tied with big red ribbons. Between two buildings, a man was selling Christmas trees, and holiday music from his radio filled the air.

Bobby paused, looked up and motioned to Poofin that he was going into the store. It took Bobby fifteen minutes to select the presents. Stepping out onto the sidewalk, he was amazed to see that a large crowd had gathered.

"I don't believe it." someone shouted.

"No one will buy those trees now," somebody else said.

"My business is ruined!" cried the owner of the Christmas trees.

Bobby slowly made his way to the front of the crowd. At first he couldn't believe his eyes. All the Christmas trees were now at least 35 feet tall.

"They're too big to put in a house," everyone agreed.

Bobby looked upward and spotted Poofin looking down at all the people. He looked very pleased with himself. He thought he had done something good even though he didn't see any of the people smiling.

"Poofin, listen to me," Bobby called," people can't use these Christmas trees now. They are too big for our houses. Bigger is not better, even though you probably thought so. Please make the Christmas trees the same size as they were."

Poofin understood. He sadly closed his eyes.

"Oh, my!" the crowd said in unison as the trees began to shrink to their normal size. "Thank goodness!" exclaimed the Christmas tree owner.

"Thank-you, Poofin ... let's go home," said Bobby.

In his room, Bobby talked quietly with Poofin, reassuring him that he knew Poofin's intentions had been good. Changing the size of the Christmas trees just wasn't a practical idea.

"Why, we would have to change the size of all our houses," Bobby thought out loud. Then he saw Poofin start to smile. "No, no, don't even think of it, Poofin," said Bobby. "No one wants their house any different, not one little bit."

"Maybe there is something else you can do ..." Bobby didn't finish the sentence. He had fallen asleep.

Mr. Brown always met in the morning with the children who were going to lead or ride his animals in the Christmas procession. As Bobby approached Mr. Brown's main gate, he could see other children and some parents inside the fence. The wail of crying children and the "Oh no's" of upset parents combined to make an awful chorus.

First he spotted Mr. Brown sitting on a large boulder, his head in his hands, and he too was crying.

"I can't look ... I can't look anymore," he moaned.

The tearful children continued to sob and their parents stared in disbelief. There were Mr. Brown's animals ... no, they really weren't exactly his animals. Carla, Corrine and Carol were standing together. Before, each camel had two humps. Now they didn't even have one! Willie, the pig and his brothers and sisters now were covered with feathers. Harriet, Mr. Brown's favorite cow, wore a coat of fluffy white wool. All the animals were changed in one way or another. And they all looked terribly sad.

"Oh, no, no, no," said Bobby, and he too began to cry. He couldn't look into Carla's sorrowful eyes another moment. He turned and ran for home.

Bobby rushed into his room and threw himself, sobbing, on the bed.

"What is the matter, Bobby?" Poofin asked softly. "I have a surprise for you. I think you will like it." Poofin had returned and was once again floating above Bobby's desk.

When he had heard Poofin's voice, Bobby quickly sat up. "Oh, Poofin, if your surprise concerns Mr. Brown's animals, it is no surprise and I don't like it."

Poofin looked confused and a little afraid. "I thought that since people change their clothes that Mr. Brown's animals would like to change and wear different coats, too. Wasn't that a good idea?"

"No, Poofin," Bobby said gently. "I'm sorry, but that wasn't a good idea. It was a very bad idea. Animals do not want to change. There is a reason why some animals have fur and others skin or feathers. They are content with their shapes and their sizes. You have made Mr. Brown, his animals and all the children very unhappy. They are still crying. Please go back to Mr. Brown's farm and change the animals back to the way they were."

Poofin was crushed ... everything he did was wrong. He felt discouraged and spiritless. His efforts had only made things worse. Heartbroken, he drifted out of the window towards Mr. Brown's farm.

Late in the evening, Bobby, dressed like a Wise Man, went with his parents to Mr. Brown's farm. All the animals had been changed back to the way they had always looked. Mr. Brown, the children and parents were happy.

It was a cold night. On a table near the gate, some parents were pouring hot chocolate. Each child was taken by Mr. Brown to an animal. Every child carried a gift which would be given to children in hospitals or to poor families on Christmas day. The parents kissed their children good-bye. They would wait on top of the hill.

Mr. Brown and his helpers, who were dressed like shepherds, quickly led the costumed children and their animals to their places in the procession. Strong hands gently picked Bobby up and placed him on Carla's back between her two humps.

Mr. Brown went first, leading a donkey which carried a woman wearing a long white robe.

On top of the hill a large crowd was gathered around Mr. McGonigal's stable. Each person held a lighted candle. As more and more people arrived, the hill began to glow.

Below, the procession silently wound its way through the streets.

Sitting on Carla's back, Bobby was the first to see how beautiful the shining hill looked in the distance. Stars sparkled like diamonds in the almost clear night sky. Only a solitary small white cloud floated above Mr. Brown and the children.

It was almost midnight by the time the procession began to climb the hill. Hundreds of voices welcomed them, singing Christmas carols.

Mr. Brown helped the woman off the donkey and they both entered the creche. The woman held a baby in her arms and the children began taking their presents one by one to the manger. Bobby sat quietly on Carla, watching and waiting his turn.

Poofin was watching too. He was very, very sad. He had grown to love Bobby and all the people of Peacedale. He had learned the reason for and the true meaning of giving but had been unable to contribute anything to this wonderful night. He had never felt so sad. He began to cry.

It was so cold that Poofin's tears immediately turned to large snowflakes which slowly drifted down onto the creche. As his sobbing increased, the snow came down faster and faster! People raised their heads and began to smile and then hug each other. It was snowing again in Peacedale!

Bobby, too, had looked up. "Poofin, Poofin," he shouted," what a wonderful gift you are giving us. We have wanted snow for so long... you are making everyone so happy!"

At first Poofin could hardly believe Bobby's words. Then his feelings changed from sorrow to joy, but he continued to cry... only now they were tears of happiness!

After the final gift was placed in the manger, families began to leave. Everyone thought how lovely it was to walk in the soft silence of falling snow.

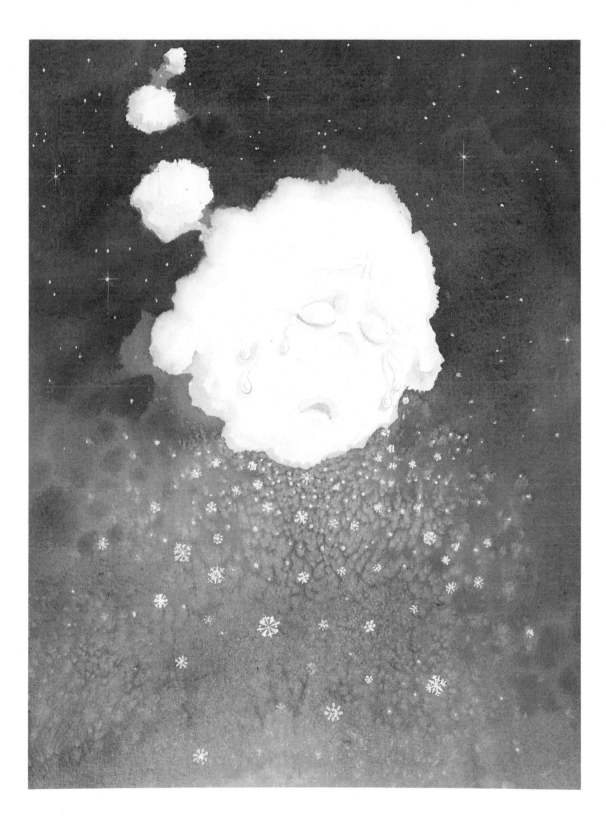

The following morning Bobby awoke early. Bright sunlight streamed in his window. He had left the window open a crack, hoping Poofin would return. Looking outside the window, Bobby gasped with delight. Deep snow covered the ground as far as one could see.

Bobby dressed quickly. He couldn't wait to try out the old sled that had belonged to his father. His father had kept it like new and each year had placed it on the porch at Christmas, hoping for snow.

Standing on the porch, Bobby looked up at the blue sky. It was clear except for a small white angelic cloud that was slowly rising higher and higher.

Bobby leaped from the porch into the soft snow. "Poofin, Poofin, please come back," he called. But the tiny cloud continued to climb higher. Tears began to roll down Bobby's cheeks. His friend was disappearing.

Bobby could hear the laughter of children and their parents who were sledding and making snow men on Apple Hill. For a moment they paused as the murmur of a gentle breeze floated over their heads.

Poofin spoke: "Bobby, thanks to you I have learned about the earth and its people. I know there are many ways I can help and will spend my life looking for places and people that need me."

Bobby brushed away a tear. "Will you ever return to us, Poofin?" Bobby asked.

And Bobby never forgot Poofin's final words: "Yes, Bobby, I will return every Christmas ... I promise!"

YEARS WENT BY... Bobby grew up, married and had a family of his own. Each year he told the story of Poofin's visit to his children and later to his grandchildren. Everyone loved the story of the little white cloud. Sometimes the children wondered if it was a made-up, imaginary story. Yet they knew that as long as they had lived in Peacedale, it always snowed on Christmas!

The
End